The Oddity

THE ODDITY

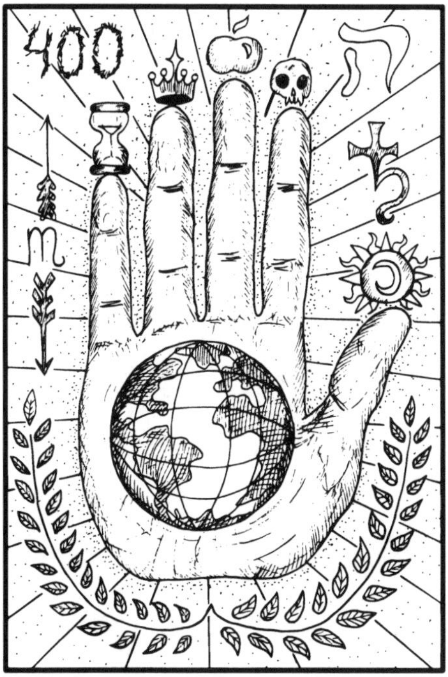

KAT HAWTHORNE

CDP

Published 2016 by Common Deer Press

First edition published in 2014 by MuseIt Up Publishing
This edition published in 2016 by Common Deer Press.

Library of Congress Cataloging-in-Publication Data
Hawthrone, Kat.--First edition.
The Oddity / Kat Hawthorne

ISBN 978-0-9950729-2-3 (print)
ISBN 978-0-9950729-3-0 (e-book)

Cover Image: © samiramay Adobe Stock
Design by: Ellie Sipila www.movetothewrite.com

Printed in the United States of America

www.commondeerpress.com

CDP

To my grandmother, Ruth, who is responsible for my weirdness.

1

The Hanged Man

♥♦♣♠

The Hanged Man dangled precariously from his right ankle rather than his neck, which would have been more prudent, not to mention effective. His clothing from another time suggested someone of noble, or at least better-than-average birth. It was difficult to tell if the expression on his face was a grimace of pain or a sneer of indignation or perhaps just a hefty dose of stomach upset. The tree he was affixed to appeared vibrant and well and had all the classic fittings of age and wisdom. Indeed, even the neatly tied noose seemed to be in good spirits, if such a thing can be said of a rope.

The Hanged Man does not necessarily mean death," said the card-reading witch sitting opposite me. The lilt of her words was unusual, suggesting a different generation rather than a different heritage. Slowly, she unfurled a single, spindly finger from her tightly closed fist and scratched it over the card's worn surface with the sort of confidence that came from extreme familiarity. "The Hanged Man is the card of the paradox. A great change is coming. Immense joy will be had, but not until an equal sacrifice is made."

I sighed inwardly, for as with everything else in this bloody room, that made absolutely no sense whatsoever. "But what can I sacrifice that is the equivalent of death?"

"You are not listening," cackled the witch. Her voice sounded like feet over broken glass. "I said death might not be the intent of this card. But since you asked, death is equal to death, and so is life."

I sighed and took a moment to wonder why I'd bothered to come here—to waste these precious few remaining hours with this shriveled piece of jerky rather than with a fine red of either the liquid or the female kind. Either would have been fine. "But to give my life or my death is to defeat the purpose," I said, which was the truth. The two were one and the same. If I were to offer either, none of this would matter for I'd be dead.

The witch had the audacity to shrug, as if my life meant that little to her. "While it may be true that your mortality is one thing you can give, it is not all that you have."

With mighty, hard won effort, I resisted the urge to slap my heavily bejewelled hand across the witch's cryptic mouth. "That is not true," I growled, my frustration trumping my good breeding. I needed answers, not this hog swill.

"The Hanged Man desires a sacrifice from within, child," she said, tapping her hairless temple in case I was unsure of the term *within*. "The sacrifice will not be easy; simplicity is not the point. What do you have that you hold dear but serves little purpose? That should be the first to go." Her eyes were rheumy with age, which gave them a strange vagueness, but still, she managed to look at me as if I were the stupidest animal on the planet.

I turned each of my rings round and round my fingers in turn, wondering what in the name of the Devil I had that I didn't need. I shifted my position on the uncomfortable chair, my seat bones starting to ache. The chair's soft wood jeered in a way that sounded like either laughter or ass music.

The tiny, ill-lit room was every bit as shoddy as the woman who owned it. It stank of mold and unwashed bodies—or dead ones. The embers in the small fireplace did little to illuminate anything, which was something I was not entirely ungrateful for. Full light would have meant I'd have to look at the details of the witch's craggy face. That likely would have turned my stomach.

"I don't understand the question," I said eventually. "I've already given up so much. I simply can't do with any less." Besides, I had come here to gain information, not to give something away.

"Vanity, haughtiness, pride, pompousness… Who knows. You must look at yourself from the viewpoint of another." She glared at me, only the look was not angry. Her eyes glinted with either laughter or age, I really couldn't tell which. "Let us look at another card. Perhaps that will give us further insight."

2

The Tower

♥♦♣♠

A cold hand touched her forehead. "Darling," said the familiar voice. "What have you Seen?"

Katasuma rolled onto her back, blinking in the flickering fingertip of candlelight her father held in his shaking hand. It was not yet morning, the room still invisible beyond the lighted circle. She yawned. "Good morning, Papa."

Her father smiled, his thin face stretching thinner still. "Did you sleep well?"

Katasuma nodded then sat up, her mass of black hair sticking to the back of her neck. "I Saw the Emperor becoming ill after eating the partridge at dinner tonight," she said.

Low sat up a little taller. "Attempted poisoning?"

Katasuma shook her head. "Bad cooking."

Low sighed. "The man is a wretch. Why does he insist on cooking his own food?" The question was rhetorical. Everyone knew that the Emperor enjoyed experimenting in the kitchen despite the number of times he suffered for it. "And that is all?"

It was difficult for Katasuma to remember her Visions. They often came at night when she was in the part of sleep that was not yet dreaming but not fully awake, either. Over the years she had taken to writing them down, although sometimes her penmanship left something to be desired—like today. She squinted at the letters. Even she could barely read it. "I have Seen the Emperor lose at dice to Lord Flynn," she said finally.

Low chuckled. "Again," he said.

Katasuma grinned. "I can tell you what Lady Marin will be wearing today if you wish to complement her."

Low made a noise in the back of his throat that sounded like either a mouse in its final death throws or a reprimand. "You know I cannot do such a thing," he said. "I am obligated to dress in my official robes as the Emperor tells me."

Katasuma knew all too well that the Emperor liked to control everything, including the colour and style of robes his advisors wore. Katasuma looked at her father's bony hands. "You ought to retire, Papa. We could buy a holding of our own where you will be free to wear what you want."

Low stood, taking up the candle again. His already craggy face appeared even gaunter when lit from below. "I would like nothing more, but I cannot provide for you outside of the Temple." He stood with no small degree of difficulty. He patted her cheek. His hand was cold. "I will return soon with your breakfast." He straightened as much as he could and retreated toward the door in his strange, humping gait. He made no noise as he left aside from the muffled drag and hop that came as his leather covered feet sputtered over the uneven stone floor.

Normally, Katasuma went back to sleep after making her report to her father.

But today, she lay on her back and stared at a ceiling she could not see, thinking.

She knew her father was right—they could never leave the Temple. Theirs was a unique circumstance that required extreme care. They could not afford to be heedless, for if Katasuma were ever discovered, the results were sure to be disastrous. Oddities were supposed to be extinct, the cull long over, and as far as Katasuma knew, she was the only one still alive. Her father, having hidden her all these years—how many years was it? Fifteen? Sixteen? She didn't rightly know—was now a criminal because of it. Treason of this sort would unquestioningly result in death for both of them.

Low was getting old, that was no secret. Although she couldn't guess at the amount of time he had left, Katasuma doubted it was very long—she had Seen his death. Despite the fact that it was possible to change the future—Katasuma and her father did it everyday by giving advanced warnings—it was not possible to stop death.

Aside from the excruciating sadness that would come with losing her father, Katasuma knew her own life would be in great jeopardy upon his death too. She depended on him for food, clothing, companionship. She lived in his rooms—rooms that would be given to someone else when he was gone. She had no other way of earning a living—nowhere else to go. No knowledge, even, of how to go about leaving. She'd never been beyond her father's chamber door.

Katasuma took a shuddering breath and rolled onto her side. This problem consumed her every waking thought.

The way she saw it, she had two choices. She could either take to the streets on her own where she understood young women in her situation were not treated particularly kindly, or she could turn herself in and face a lifetime of enslavement or, more likely, execution. "I will have to think of something," she said to the dark.

Later that morning, when Low returned with the breakfast of bread and tea—his own rations that he shared with her—he brought something unexpected.

"What is it?" Katasuma asked, although the answer became obvious when he handed it to her.

"It's a book," he said. "It seems to me that you spend too much time alone. I thought this might be a way for you to occupy your time."

Katasuma grinned in such a way as to show even her back teeth.

She consumed the book at such a rate, she soon needed another. And another. And as many as Low could carry back to her without raising suspicion. Her favourites were the ones that spoke of damsels trapped in towers or treated as slaves by wicked relatives, especially when they ended with the damsel's liberation and bloody revenge. She enjoyed the medical texts that contained hand-drawn images of the insides of human bodies, and took to tracing the pictures, searching for a solution to her father's illness though she never found one. She read textbooks about history, though those didn't interest her much. Still, on occasion she would be rewarded with a wonderful story about scandal or bloodlust, which made the reading more tolerable.

But more than any of that, Katasuma hungered for information about Fisk, the creator of the Oddity experiments. Those books, however, were hard to come by, for the Emperor had had most of them burned along with their heretic author.

She'd first heard about Fisk while reading a dull volume of clipped newspaper articles. She was just about to close the book when she came across a small square of paper that looked out of place. It was yellowed and frail, half its words smeared across the page as if it had been wet at some point.

Katasuma hunkered closer to it, as if getting closer would make the reading easier. It didn't.

> ...Oddity with the ability to call upon the rain. In this unprecedented success, Fisk has truly outdone himself, for what could be better in the midst of a drought than a great showering of rain? When asked what he planned next, Fisk answered, "I think I should like to develop an...

Katasuma could not make out any more words.

3

The Hermit

♥♦♣♠

Everything about The Hermit looked haggard. His cloak hung limply from his skeletal frame, tattered and in obvious need of severe laundering. His beard hung halfway down his scrawny chest, scraggly and grey, signifying great age if not an abundance in hygiene. In his hand he clutched an archaic-looking lamp that did a fine job of illuminating absolutely nothing, which was what surrounded him.

"Splendid," I grumbled while sighing deeply. So much can be said through the deepness of a sigh.

"I should think so as well," said the witch, with an uneven smirk. "You have a great journey ahead of you, although this journey will require no packing. All that you know, or all that you think you know, are but trifling urges, flawed and unclear due to your own primitive ideas and private circumstances. The Hermit seeks true knowledge, which I daresay is something not overly abundant in you at the present time." The witch looked at the table and said so quietly I almost couldn't hear, "This will be a long journey, or so I would suspect."

I frowned but showed my good breeding by overlooking the insult in favour of far more serious issues, such as the possibility of my imminent death. "Will this long journey that requires no packing consist of my soul traversing into the next world?" I asked, trying to make the question as simple as possible, for obviously this ancient fiend was slight on sensibilities.

"I cannot answer that," she answered, as if I'd just asked the most ridiculous question she'd ever heard. She continued cackling for a moment longer, although I couldn't guess at what she found so damned funny. However, when she finally collected herself and continued speaking, it was with seriousness. "All I can tell you with any certainty is what the cards have revealed. I am a translator, nothing more."

The witch's hooked claw traced the outline of the card. "The Hermit's lessons often have to do with material things and the way we tend to define ourselves by what we do or do not have rather than what we are or are not. He encourages the value of the internal, for he knows physical things are not meant to last and mean little when compared with the universe. Consider it a quest if that suits your noble tastes, but this quest does not involve riches of the sparkly kind. Ultimate power comes with the knowledge that everything you will ever need is already within you."

And that was a grand speech coming from someone smelling of old chamber pots. "I haven't the luxury of time to seek anything, witch," I said, not bothering to conceal my contempt. "I am scheduled to swing in just over a week."

At some point during my terribly clever answer, the witch's grin, which had previously been more mischievous than genuine, changed into something serious indeed. "You've answered your own question," she said slyly, as if that made any sense. "If time is the answer, all you must do is create more time."

It seemed to me as if the witch was speaking in a foreign language, for what she said was vague and could be construed in countless ways. I chuffed a disgruntled breath through my teeth, which created a satisfying yet unexpected hissing sound. "You are talking nonsense, old woman."

"You are thinking only of limitations." She rapped her gnarled monkey knuckles across the scarred tabletop as if to demonstrate the meaning of the word *limitation.*

"But knowledge has the power to transcend all that." Her hands slithered off the table bonelessly and thudded into her lap. "You must acknowledge your faults and use that destructive energy in more beneficial ways. If you are willing to learn, there are no limitations, boy. Your body will die one day no matter how hard you try to deny it. Time is terminal, the greatest killer anyone has ever known. But physical death is not what's important. The soul is eternal. It's what you do with your time that determines who you are and what you are capable of. That is what you will carry with you."

I heard the witch mutter something on either side of the word "buffoon," which clearly couldn't have been in relation to me. She was obviously delusional.

Then, with a flourish surprisingly nimble for someone of her advanced age, the witch flipped the next card, jarring me back into the present.

4

The Magician

♥♦♣♠

"I think you may find this of interest, darling," Low said to his daughter, taking a dusty book from inside his cloak. "Although preserving this for you nearly cost me my life, I have always known there would be a time that you would need to see it. No one besides me knows it exists."

Katasuma took the book, which was warm from her father's skin. The leather binding cracked and snapped as she opened it, the smell of ink huffing into her face. The paper was thin, the words scratched in a sweeping scrawl, but the book did not seem particularly old. Just neglected.

The title read: *The Criminal Trial of Lord Fisk.*

Katasuma gasped. "I thought all the records about Fisk were destroyed."

Slowly, Low shuffled across the grand seating room to his favourite chair that sat next to the fire. He groaned as he lowered himself into it, taking care to bend his shoddy knee gradually. Katasuma walked to her customary place beside him and sat on the floor near the hearth to get a better look at what she was holding.

"They were all destroyed, quite right, my dear. All except this one, which I stowed away for you." Low said with a bit of cheek. "The journal in the back was used as evidence in Lord Fisk's trial."

Katasuma began reading immediately.

Fisk was young when he'd begun conceptualizing the Oddity experiments—likely around Katasuma's current age. Originally, the experiments had been devised as a currency of sorts, because even though Fisk's family was very wealthy, and he had grown up with every luxury anyone could ever desire, Fisk famously enjoyed a bit of impish fun and was forever getting into trouble with the law.

Alongside the legal documents outlining his misdeeds were hand written accounts of the devilry by Fisk himself. One such well-documented event told of Fisk breaking into the local printing press late one night and rearranging a portion of the letter stamps so that the next day when the printers were run, half the words came out back to front. From what Katasuma could see, judging by his criminal record, Fisk was hotheaded and perhaps a little pompous, but had a great heart for fun, as rarely were his crimes any more serious than good-natured naughtiness.

However, despite his love for merrymaking, there was one seemingly uncharacteristic instance that was very serious indeed. Shortly before he began working on his experiments, Fisk was arrested in connection with aiding a known criminal—a man by the name of Terek who was rumoured to have plotted against the Emperor. As a result, Fisk was charged, found guilty of treason, and sentenced to hang, which fueled his need for immediate enlightenment and resulted in several schemes to save his life. He was granted two weeks to set his affairs to rights, which was a luxury he was afforded thanks to the depths of his father's well-lined pockets.

Of course, Fisk tried to use his remaining time to free himself of his grave situation. He hired some commoners to clean the city streets, but he did none of the work himself. He offered to pay the medical expenses of those who could not afford their own care, only the money was not his to spend. He asked his cooks to prepare far more food than was necessary, offering the left over meals to the hungry, only to leave them hungry again the following day. Fisk did not understand that by sacrificing little, there was little to gain, and his meager efforts had had no effect on the law.

Finally, in a desperate act, Fisk turned to the talents of a card-reading witch for guidance. Although the practice was considered blasphemy, Fisk was in dire need of inspiration and had nowhere left to go. And that was where he found the answers he had been searching for.

The idea of developing an army of unnaturally clever and burly soldiers to bulk up the Emperor's dwindling infantry at a time when the nation was perpetually on the brink of war was to become his salvation. According to his records, Fisk worked tirelessly on the "Limitless" concept and neither slept nor ate for an entire week prior to his scheduled date with the hangman. Fisk's thoughts abounded way beyond the confines of natural human thought, his despair aiding in his open- mindedness. So, because he wanted to remain among the living, during what was meant to be the final week of his life, Fisk devised a plan to buy his liberation.

On the day of his scheduled execution, when asked if he had any final words, Fisk calmly replied, "Yes, thank you. I wish to tell the Emperor that I have developed a way to guarantee his most deserved victory on the battlefield. If I may, I'd like to present my idea for consideration, for if he allows it, what I propose is guaranteed to save our fine nation. Then, when prosperity is restored and peace has befallen the land, I shall fulfill my sentence and you may see me swing if it still suits you, my good man."

The crowd gathered at the base of the scaffolding to witness the execution stood in silent amazement. Typically before the completion of their sentence, the condemned would spend their final breaths confessing their mortal sins and pleading for forgiveness and salvation. But not Fisk. Fisk had a nobler purpose, or so it must have seemed.

Astonished and undoubtedly intrigued, the Emperor accepted Fisk's proposal. Shortly thereafter, Fisk began working on the promised solution under the employ of the royal family who wanted the concept brought to fruition as quickly as possible for obvious reasons.

So, in order to fulfill his promise to the Emperor, Fisk hastily concocted the serum he had devised while imprisoned. It didn't take long, just some trial and error. Then he injected the Emperor's already trained soldiers with his serum, and after a few failed attempts and unusual reactions, he managed to create something with fairly dependable results. Within a relatively short amount of time, Fisk's renovated soldiers were firmly in possession of much greater physical bulk, increased stamina, prominent aggression, remarkably good health, and incurable loyalty to the crown.

And all this was very well and good and did wonderful things to guarantee Fisk's otherwise questionable longevity, but really, Fisk had little interest in the physical size and attitudes of the military men. Secretly, he had used this experiment as a forerunner for something much more extraordinary. He knew that if he could learn to tweak specific physical characteristics with accuracy, there was no reason why he shouldn't be able to engineer cognitive abilities, too, possibly exploiting those well beyond the natural abilities of a human.

5

The Ace of Swords

♥♦♣♠

The Ace of Swords looked majestic and worthy of a person of my station. Like the most spectacular phallus, the solitary weapon stood tall and strong, its gleaming hilt sunk deep into the gripping palm of a disembodied hand. A crown balanced on its tip, brilliantly decorated with undeterminable riches. Surely this had to represent greatness and upward mobility, which made sense when considering me. I couldn't repress the grin that spread across my face, not that I wanted to repress anything. Obviously the other two cards and all the talk of journeys and sacrifices had been incorrectly interpreted through the mouth of an ass.

But upon seeing it, the witch's leathery forehead collected in a deep scowl. She grunted indelicately, as if considering something terribly difficult. I had no doubt that considering anything at all was likely terribly difficult for the witch, but still, it was disconcerting.

"Well, this is confirmation of a change," she began, her voice dour and serious. "But you must proceed with caution. The Sword is capable of many great things, but it is double-edged—its wielder in a very perilous position indeed. Make the right choice, and the sword will allow you to achieve all you've ever dreamed of. However, choose poorly and it could be your undoing, as it will just as easily slice off your insignificant head."

I grunted, because it was the only response I was capable of for a short while. Then, remembering to be insulted, I said, "My head is most definitely not insignificant, witch." The statement held very little conviction however, which made the claim seem untrue. Considering the dwindling number of hours I had left with my mortality, it seemed the witch was not the only one who thought my head trivial.

The witch grinned toothlessly once again, and the expression was wholly gruesome. "I do believe you are beginning to understand," she said in a far jollier tone than the occasion called for. "That is what I have been trying to tell you, boy. You do not need your head at all! In itself, your head means little. You simply need what is within it, assuming you are interested in using the power of this card for beneficial purposes rather than destructive ones?"

I nodded in response. The truth of it was, I had no idea what, exactly, I wanted beyond the chance to live a little longer. The state of my head seemed rather important when placed in the context of my survival, but I wasn't about to argue.

The witch resumed her interpretation. "The Ace of Swords marks the beginning of all that lies ahead, although it gives no indication of the outcome. It has great duality. This card tells us that you have the ability to achieve whatever it is that you wish for; however, it does not tell if the result will help or hinder you."

"Useless," I muttered, maybe at the card, maybe at the witch. Either seemed relevant.

"Not at all, boy, unless you allow it to become so." The witch's tone was disturbing in its sweetness. "This is an opportunity to show the Emperor that your death will be a mistake. You have some ideas moving about? Now is the time to act."

She was entirely correct in her assumption that I had some ideas. I had lots of ideas—more ideas than she'd probably had in her whole life. But ideas were of little value to a person who would not have the time to develop them. "I don't have time for ideas," I said truthfully.

"You're right," she said. "You have already decided that you are going to die, and therefore that is what you should expect. You are creating that future for yourself by being obtuse. This card would not have presented itself if there was no possibility for your salvation, boy, unless death itself will be that salvation."

The witch's glare was so intense it felt as if she were trying to see the other side of the room by looking through my head rather than by using the conventional-method. "Are you reading my mind, witch?" I said, for I'd heard the rumours.

"Yes," she said, grinning.

6

The High Priestess

♥♦♣♠

According to Fisk's firsthand records, years went by before he started work on what would, in Katasuma's time, be considered the greatest example of sacrilege committed by a mortal ever recorded. For Fisk's true work did not have much to do with taking what already existed and compounding it into something similar or slightly better as he had done for the soldier's serum. No, Fisk's dream was to create something where previously there had been nothing.

However, progress was agonizingly slow. According to many sullen accounts in his diary, Fisk quickly discovered that taking an idea and transforming it into a reality took more than mere intelligence. He spent a good long while testing and questioning and basically disrupting any concept he had of mortal limitations, for what he wanted to achieve could not be defined by its limits. And it looked well on paper; his ideas were clearly thought out and developed down to the smallest detail. But, unfortunately, bringing those ideas into practice was another matter altogether.

Theories. Fisk had lots of them. For example:

Dilution

I've had a new thought of late that is far too ingenious to overlook. Granted, I have thoughts of this impressive magnitude on a regular basis, but I believe this may be the answer for which I've been searching.

In chemistry, dilution is the act of making something weaker. Indeed, dilution is something I became very good fellows with while creating the stinking Emperor's serum. Generally, the term refers to a liquid—adding something toan otherwise potent mixture to make it more manageable. And this is all fine and well, but I am not terribly interested in liquid, unless, of course, it has a fine vintage and has recently come from the distillery. And even then, it has to be something really special to hold my interest. Well, something fairly special. Or something halfway decent at the least.

What I am talking about is dilution in the context of time.

The witch goes on and on no end about the meaninglessness of the human body, claiming that it is the soul that is eternal, the soul we should concern ourselves with maintaining. Of course, all her chatter is very tiresome and does little beyond causing my irritation to peak, but for reasons I will never understand, I listen to her anyway, somewhat fond of her zany observations, which never fail to raise a laugh. However, if what she says is true and the human body is naught but a vehicle for the ever-present soul, what, exactly, does that mean?

Of all the illnesses and all that plagues the human body, time is the most dangerous. Eventually, we are all beat by time—there is no stopping it. What I've been pondering is a way to dilute time, in effect, slowing it down, weakening it, allowing a body to live, potentially, forever. Time is the pathway to divinity, for it could be said that the one who controls time controls life and death, and the one who controls life and death transcends the realm of mortality and enters into the realm of the Gods.

I am going to find a way to dilute time.

Katasuma closed the book with a hearty thud then opened it again. It was late—or early, depending on how you looked at it—and she should have been sleeping hours before, but she couldn't stop. Lord Fisk was insane.

It was difficult to tell in some instances which of the theories made it beyond the concept stage and into the developmental one, but some of the earliest entries were easy to identify within the first generation of successful Oddities.

For example, there was a great deal of time and space spent in Fisk's journals devoted to memories. Fisk believed, or so it seemed, that memories had the ability to call the events of the past into the future. Among the first wave of Oddities he produced were individuals capable of recalling a person's past—any person at all—and materializing a portion of that past into the present day. It was not necromancy; the Oddities with this particular skill could not revive anything deceased (that would come later in another strain of Oddities not yet developed at the time of this entry), but there were instances recorded of old warriors who had once been brave and courageous on the battlefield that had either been injured or had aged past the point of usefulness suddenly becoming able to perform certain tasks again thanks to the talents of these Oddities.

Naturally, Oddities with this skill were cast into the healing arts—both mental and physical. Restoring vitality back into the old and bravery back into the cowardly was something miraculous indeed. However, as time went by and it was discovered that increased belief in one's physical wellbeing did not equal an actual mending—it was merely a placebo-like façade—the skill was downgraded to mere illusion.

There were other early examples of successful Oddities that had the ability to adjust their weight, lightening themselves until they were able to climb to the very tip of even the spindliest tree or scale vertical walls using nothing more than bits of moss for leverage. Or, alternately, these Oddities were capable of becoming so heavy they could not be moved by even the most powerful of the Emperor's prized strong-arms. These particular Oddities, of course, were fantastic spies, for they could get into impossible places using little more than a stiff wind to heft them, or they could crush holes in great walls by running and flinging themselves, therefore making passage possible where it otherwise would not have been, at least not without a great effort and amount of time spent.

Katasuma had always been curious to know, of course, about her own skill. She was the only Oddity she knew of who had ever been granted the ability to look into the future. But she didn't understand, for example, why she could See some things but not others. She wondered if her skill was somewhat flawed, or perhaps if she was just not strong enough to use it properly. Searching for the answer kept her reading until she found this:

Decisions

During my reading, the witch spoke some utter nonsense about the way desires affect the future. Of course, what she said was moronic and more than likely the result of an evening spent with a full pipe and lack of common sense, but for someone as active-witted as I, what she said made a strange sense. Her claim was that, if we truly believe in a thing with complete conviction, without the slightest trace of doubt, unwaveringly, faithfully, it is possible to bring that belief into fact.

She had no idea, of course, what she was saying; half soused and cackling like a lunatic, as is her usual custom, or so I understand. But still, disguised as it was in simpleminded gibberish, it sparked in me the desire to know more. I found I could not ignore the concept, for my mind is a fertile vessel forever lusting after knowledge. Simply put, I could not rest until I knew the truth behind the claim.

And now, after some lengthy consideration, my theory is as follows: if a firm decision is made within a person's mind, that decision must indeed be real in some way. We can see ourselves doing the decided upon thing, we can see the outcome. So how, I ask, would we be able to see a thing if it did not exist? Perhaps it is not as obvious as an item we can pick up and hold, but once a decision is made, the event does exist somewhere, even if it is within another realm. I intend to find the connection between absolute decisions and their affect on our reality.

Katasuma scratched her head, wishing her father were awake to discuss this with. The idea did not describe exactly any specific skill that Katasuma was familiar with—it seemed more the vague possibility of a skill rather than the description of one. But it made a strange sense to Katasuma that decisions really ought to be more tangible than they were.

And then she got to thinking. If this theory could be related to her own skill, it would explain quite a bit. If she were Seeing decisions as they were made, and taking into consideration the fickleness of the human mind, it would explain why she couldn't See everything, and why some things she did See never came to be. People could change their minds, but there was no way to erase a vision from Katasuma after she'd seen it.

Likewise, if a person acted without thinking the action through, wouldn't that explain the surprises in life? Hence the future she could not predict.

Katasuma scanned the theory again and then once more after that, and as she did, it made more and more sense. She was not Seeing the future. Oh no. What she was seeing were the decisions people made as they made them.

7

Temperance

♥♦♣♠

The angel on the Temperance card was a welcome sight. In complete contrast to the shredded garb of The Hermit, Temperance looked strong and well and virtuously tidy. He held a sword in one hand and a cup in the other, both fine riches indicative of excellent social status. His feathered wings, open and powerful, were stained red, which seemed an unusual colour choice but not unpleasant. His bare feet held ground atop a pool of depthless, wavy water.

"My guardian?" I asked, hopeful. I looked up at the witch and was surprised to be met with the clarity of wisdom in her eyes.

She paused a moment before she answered. "This is the point during which you become who you truly are.

You have been through some trials, and you will go through some more, but now you may take strength knowing that Temperance awaits. You must accept your fears, your worries, your doubts. Identify them all, for by claiming them, they can no longer hold power over you."

"What do you mean?" I asked, genuinely interested. I shuffled my feet impatiently.

The witch traced her finger around the edge of the card, as if its frayed texture belonged to something alive. "It's simple in concept but difficult in practice."

I nodded, trying to maintain my patience. "Yes, yes, of course. Go on."

"You fear death, but you empower it by giving it the energy of your fear. You must accept the fact that death will come for you no matter what you do. So see it not with negativity, but acceptance. There is no point in wasting your energy being afraid of something you cannot control. Tell me, are you a spiritual man?"

It seemed to be contrary to her position as a card-reading witch to be concerned with religion, but if she wanted to know if I'd spent my share of time in church, deadening the sensation in my knees while confessing my sins again and again, reciting hymns and verses from another time that seemed to say little to me, then the answer was yes. I had done those things. But I was quite certain that she was not asking if I'd paid my penitence within the church walls, making right with my maker before my day of Reckoning. Still, "Yes," I said, but even as I said it, it sounded like a lie.

The witch let the word hang in the air. Finally, she continued. "And you are happy with your level of suffering?"

I scoffed hollowly. "Who is happy to suffer?"

The witch nodded vigorously causing some hidden accessory to tinkle. "Exactly right. And yet, you call it upon yourself. By choosing to fear, you are choosing to suffer. Likewise, by feeling guilt at your lack of spiritual conviction, you are choosing to suffer. There is no right or wrong answer to my question, child. There is no right or wrong answer to anything. There is simply suffering and not suffering, and that is different for everyone. But, by stripping power away from the things that cause you pain or worry or regret or guilt, you will become stronger in your happiness."

This made a strange sense to me. "I should not fear death, for death is not the end," I said simply. "And fearing it allows it to manifest within me." God, it was as though I'd been possessed.

The witch clapped her hands together jovially. "Yes," she said, "you understand! But you must also accept that this will be a difficult battle to win, for it is human nature to fear the unknown. But by recognizing that physical death is inevitable and seeing the pointlessness in fearing it, you are robbing it of its power."

The witch leaned forward on her elbows, her claws digging into the table's well-worn surface. "Can you see the limitlessness now, boy? The potential of the universe is within you. Temperance calls for your strength and the purity of who you are. You can never go wrong if you remain true to your spirit. Decide to become aware of your true potential. All you have to do is decide."

And with that, she turned the next card.

8

JUDGMENT

♥♦♣♠

The Emperor heartily encouraged Fisk's experiments, for he understood the extraordinary benefits that could come with the skills his Oddities possessed. Their production was slow, however, for Fisk manually developed and adjusted them each individually. He discovered early on that these new skills could not be given to adults of his choosing as the serum had allowed; the skills had to be inborn. This meant, of course, that after an Odd child was born, it would be years before they knew if the experiment had been a success, for the skills he gave did not present themselves until the child was more intellectually developed.

After an early, and rather frightening failed experiment in which Fisk gave a half-dozen Odd children the ability to control fire, it was decided that just because he could do a thing, it did not mean he actually should. Fisk became more particular in the skills he chose, and he stopped creating several Oddities with the same skill at once. Even at the height of the experiments, there were never more than six or seven Odd children born per year, which kept their numbers relatively small and the individuals quite easy to track.

When Fisk first declared his need for willing subjects to offer their reproductive bodies for experimental purposes, there was something of an uproar. Mind you, this reaction was not caused by the fine citizens' fear for their mortal souls or concern that their children may turn out monstrous and in need of termination—no. The uproar was because they all wanted their children to be Odd.

Having a child in the family capable of a special skill was a highly sought after social position that would greatly increase a family's prestige, which was terribly important to the city's fine population.

Parents for Odd children were not selected based on marital vows but rather by genetics. Fisk devised a way to select individuals to mate according to the likely outcome of their progeny. By putting potential candidates through a battery of tests, scoring physical abilities, natural intelligence, and something he labeled

"Superlatives," which, according to his records, very few possessed, he chose males and females to breed based on correcting their weaknesses and heightening their strengths. When a pair was selected, the mating process was then scheduled and carried out via a team of trusted physicians adept in the art of artificial insemination.

Katasuma scoured through pages and pages of names, which had all been catalogued and assigned a series of numbers ranging between one and ten and linked to other names in the book. Curious to see how her father had scored, Katasuma flipped through the pages until she found the one titled, "Low the Wise."

Katasuma's father had ranked very high in the cognitive categories, his Intuition earning an eight, and his Superlatives a nine. Physically, Low had fared in the middle range, with both his Conformation and Beauty categories scoring a six. His athletic attributes left much to be desired, his Stamina at a two, and his Fitness at a four, not that Katasuma understood how such things were important with regards to reproduction. There was a fairly accurate hand sketch at the bottom of the page depicting a much younger and less hunched-over version of Low the Wise, looking altogether more vigorous than Katasuma had ever known him to be.

This information held Katasuma's interest for a moment, as did the notes below in which Fisk declared Low the Wise fit to father an Odd child. But what stoked her curiosity more was the number next to it, the identification code for his selected mating partner.

Katasuma had never known the identity of her mother. All Katasuma knew was that she had been born under unusual circumstances, and that her mother had died around the time of her birth.

With jittery hands, Katasuma flipped through the pages until she came to the one bearing her mother's code. She skimmed over her mother's ranks, interested but not consumed by the incredibly high scores she had earned in every single category. It was the sketch at the bottom of the page that caused Katasuma's vision to blur.

Similar to most of the other citizens of the city, Low the Wise had dark hair, dark eyes, and sand-coloured skin. It was a fine combination if not particularly striking. His features were dear to Katasuma, but rather exaggerated and large, especially on his narrow face. However, her mother, if the black and white sketch could be trusted, looked nothing like all the other commoners of the town.

The woman's skin, striking in its unusualness, was whiter than a patch of unmarked snow. Her features were small but proportionate, and her dense hair was darker than the center of a depthless pit and hung over her shoulders in thick cords like so many sleeping serpents.

Katasuma blinked then flipped back to her father's page to be sure she'd gotten the numbers right. Though the name was not familiar to her, there was only one woman with that colouring in the entire realm, or so she understood. One woman known for her striking beauty and generous heart. In that moment, Katasuma understood that her mother had been Kali, the Empress.

9

The Star

♥♦♣♠

A great, beaconing glow of unearthly light shone at the centre of the next card, but, frankly, my focus was on the naked woman. In each hand she held a cup, both spilling their contents: one on the ground, and one into the pool she was kneeling next to. Miraculously, her foot rested atop the water rather than within it, which seemed an artistic error to me. The earth around her looked fertile and prosperous, with an abundance of lush, green grass and even a leafy tree in the distance. The stars, which should have garnered my interest first considering the card's title—probably would have if not for the nipples—were in a circular pattern, all white save the centre one, which was blinding yellow.

The witch looked lovingly at the card, as if it were a sleeping babe content in its mother's arms. She smiled—an odd expression on her grisly face. "The Star," she announced, as if I couldn't read the title myself.

"So I see," I said, tempted to kick her under the table to get her attention—that's how lost she looked. "What does it mean?"

"There are few more positive cards than this one, boy. Especially if it comes when all hope seems lost. If your reality is dark, and you feel you have lost your way, the Star is here to shed a little light and guide you on your path."

I scoffed at her strange tenderness. "That sounds like something any circus fortune teller would say." I had to get my insult quota in for the day, plus, she was being an idiot, getting all teary eyed over a card.

She looked at me with something in her eyes that made me feel as though I'd been reprimanded. I cleared my throat decided to practice my newly learned skill of not feeling guilty over my immediate and sharp response thereby taking guilt's power away…or some other such nonsense.

The witch chuckled as if she understood what I was thinking and lifted her bony shoulders so high they touched the bottoms of her droopy earlobes, but gave no answer.

I shifted my position and tried to ignore the painful aching in my backside with marginal success. "What is it telling me to do?"

The witch shook her head. "I do not have the answer to that, I'm afraid, but I would be willing to bet that you do."

At that, I felt a strange meaty fist pounding in my chest that would have been frightening under any other circumstances. "Do you mean the experiments? Is this card encouraging me to begin the experiments?"

The witch looked at me intently, her scrutiny difficult to avoid. "I do not know what it is that you speak of, boy. But I do know that what you think you have lost, is really not lost at all. The Star does not tell me the outcome of your decisions, it only tells me that there is a decision to be made."

I leaned toward her, no longer caring about her foul breath or her tattered attire. "You have told me I must sacrifice something. You have told me I must go on a journey within my own mind. You have told me the path will be perilous, that I stand to lose a great deal, but that I should not fear that loss and accept it for the change it will bring. And now, you tell me I have earned encouragement. I have been too frightened to attempt the experiments. But I know that if I am successful, a world of potential will open before me. A vast improvement for the entire human population is within reach. Perhaps if I am able to show the Emperor…"

The witch looked at me as if seeing someone else. "Acknowledge your fears, understand their cause. Weigh the benefits versus the negatives. Is it worth it, boy, to try what you suggest?"

"It could mean my salvation," I answered. "And is salvation what you seek, or fame?"

I couldn't deny that I wanted a bit of both. But I had so much to offer, so many ideas that suddenly seemed possible. "I could present my thoughts to the Emperor before my sentence is carried out," I said, suddenly excited and for some reason desiring of the witch's approval. "Perhaps if he sees what I have to offer…"

The witch's expression was difficult to translate. "All that you have to offer is all that you can dream of. However, it is possible to have too much of a good thing, for at some point, all good things will end. You have a responsibility too, child, to know your place. Do not allow greed to overrule your good sense, for greed is a tricky monster—a master of manipulation and deception."

It seemed as if she had more to say, but rather than speaking, the witch turned my final card.

10

The Two of Cups

♥♦♣♠

No one understood the details of the Empress's death. It was assumed by most that her end, and that of her unseen offspring, had occurred during the latter stages of pregnancy, for the Empress's health had always been frail, and she had been constantly ill while carrying the child. No one could argue the possibility, for the Empress—who was normally very sociable—had been confined to bed rest while pregnant. No one saw her near the end, save her personal physician, whom the Emperor had executed in a rage after his wife's death.

The problem with this explanation was that the Emperor was sterile. Speculation abounded about the child's paternity, but the Emperor offered no explanation.

He preached his wife's virtues constantly, claiming the child was his. No one dared argue with him.

Naturally, rumours developed and flourished, describing late night trysts and lewd behaviour between the Empress and the bravest warriors, for the woman was extraordinarily beautiful and charming—a valuable prize for any man. Such rumours, however, were not looked upon with kindness and would earn the speaker a prison stay if overheard by the wrong set of ears, for the Emperor was very protective of his wife and forbade any ill words against her.

Whispers of a royal Oddity circulated but were soon squashed when the Emperor claimed he had forbidden such devilry to take place within the immaculate womb of his innocent wife. He said his offspring would be naturally gifted—no child of his would need help in their engineering to do spectacular things.

But then the Empress had died and the Emperor became wholly more intolerant of any speculating by the populace. In an outrage, he sentenced three men to hang simply because he could. No one ever spoke another word about the Empress and her most untimely death, or at least not where they could be overheard.

Katasuma was astounded. Suddenly, the history books that had seemed so dull before held such intrigue she lost the ability to sleep. The rumours were true! She was the Royal Oddity! The fact was almost too much for her to bear.

The Oddity experiments came to a sudden halt shortly after the Empress's death. Fisk was accused of witchery and conspiring with the Devil, which was the sentence that led to his death. A veritable cull was called, and all the Oddities were gathered and taken into custody by the imperial guard and never seen again. This was a bit of history everyone knew, for it was still somewhat fresh in the minds of the citizens.

The mothers who had taken part in the experiments would have suspected their offspring, of course, and several of them came forth of their own volition to relinquish their youngsters. They had been told that the children's lives would be spared in the custody of the Temple, which was not a promise that could be guaranteed if the children were allowed to remain free. No one knew if the Odd children gathered during that first collection were retained or exterminated, even after they claimed sanctuary.

Once the majority of the Oddities were dealt with, the Emperor passed a law legalizing the execution of anyone left in the public exhibiting Odd behaviour, for he wanted to erase the experiments altogether. No one knew with any certainty which children would actually turn out Odd, and as a result, the youngest generation—Katasuma's generation—was looked upon with extreme scrutiny by everyone around, waiting to see which of them developed a skill that suddenly seemed less special.

It was possible that other Odd children had been hidden away just as Katasuma was, although it would have been very difficult for the families to keep their secret within the Emperor's city, particularly considering the meticulous notes Fisk had kept regarding their identity and that of their parents. However, Odd or not, a child was still a child, and no one wanted to lose their children to unknown futures, which likely compelled some parents to attempt fleeing the city or hiding their babies away. Unless the families had had the foresight to flee the city before the child was born and its birth catalogued, Katasuma was certain that beyond herself, there were very few left in existence, if any at all.

It frightened Katasuma that there could be Oddities surviving in other places, for she did not know what the others were capable of. She did know, however, how difficult it was to control a powerful skill, which was something she struggled with regularly. Although it was not a direct part of her own abilities—it was more an oversight on Fisk's behalf—she knew she was capable of great destruction. It was true that she could not control the future directly—her skill had been meant for observational purposes only—but she could definitely influence the actions of the people whose futures she Saw. If she acted irresponsibly and said something to the wrong person, her intervention would set things in motion that would affect vast chains of events, causing things to occur that should not. It was too big, her skill, and she felt wholly incapable of controlling it. If there were other Oddities alive capable of similar things, it was only a matter of time before one of them made a mistake and unthinkable things happened. She only hoped she wouldn't be the one responsible.

♥♦♣♠

Early the next day, Low the Wise went into his daughter's bedchamber before the rise of the sun. "Katasuma, my darling," he said, just as he'd said every other morning of her life. "I must know what you have Seen."

Katasuma lay awake—uncommon for his daughter, who liked to sleep in. "Papa," she said with a voice more alert than he was accustomed to hearing, particularly at that hour. "I wish to know something."

It was slightly irritating for Low to be delayed in his morning ritual by the wonderings of a teenaged girl, but he adored his daughter beyond the confines of his human mind, and the slight annoyance passed by as quickly as it had arrived.

"What is it, darling?"

"I want to know how it is that you claimed me after my mother died."

Katasuma was not accustomed to speaking to people. She did not understand the need to ease in to a topic as grand as that one. Low choked on invisible things, his words thickening in his throat. "That is a very big question," he answered after collecting his wits.

"Yes," Katasuma said simply.

"Well," he sputtered. "To properly answer that, first I must..."

Katasuma sat up in her bed, allowing the blankets to fall into a wrinkly heap around her middle. The dim candlelight reflected on her face, making her features seem more extreme. "I know my mother was the Empress. I know she died sometime around my birth. I just don't understand how it is that I am here with you, that you knew I was yours, and that I did not end up dead like all the other Odd children."

Low the Wise cleared his throat, thankful for the gloom, which disguised his discomfort. He sighed deeply and nodded in the darkness. He'd known she was clever enough to figure it out—he had figured she would do so after receiving Fisk's book. He was a bit surprised, however, that she had figured it out so quickly. "Very well. Put on your robe and meet me by the fire. I will tell you all that I know."

♥♦♣♠

Low clasped his hands and braced them on his good knee. He had stirred the fire in the hearth and lit a lamp, which softened the edges of everything. He sat in his favourite chair, and Katasuma sat in hers across from him. He had never seen her more alert.

He had rehearsed this speech, wanting to say everything just right. But still, now that the time was upon him, he could scarcely find the words.

He cleared his throat. "First thing I must say is this: Katasuma, I never believed what Fisk was doing was blasphemy because his intentions were pure. He was not looking to cause destruction to us or our realm, he was looking to improve it. It was on my recommendation that the Emperor agreed to allow the experiments in the first place. In a way, I am responsible for all that has happened.

"As you obviously already know, your mother was the Empress. And I know we have always been led to believe that the two individuals selected to produce an Odd child were not supposed to know the identity of the other, and this is true for the most part. However, as you can imagine, the Emperor would not allow Kali to be matched with just anyone. This child was to become the heir to the throne. Our joining was intentional."

Katasuma pulled her legs underneath herself, her black hair loose and spilling around her shoulders, just like her mother's.

"You see, the Emperor realized shortly after his marriage to Kali that he was incapable of reproducing. He loved his wife very much, and he was frightened to tell her that he could not give her a child, for she wanted to be a mother more than anything. He asked me to do it, Kata. Lord help me, the Emperor asked me to mate with her in his stead and produce the child she so wanted. I shouldn't have deceived her, Kata, for I loved your mother, too, with all my heart."

Katasuma opened her mouth as if to speak, then closed it again.

"Fisk agreed to make you Odd, for we all expected a boy, and an Odd Emperor on the throne would be capable of so many great things. We selected your skill—Fisk devised it specially for the Empress's child, for what would be greater than a ruler who could foresee the future of his kingdom? You were to be his greatest achievement. You *are* his greatest achievement.

"But the pregnancy did not go well. Kali was a beautiful woman but as frail as a wisp of smoke. She was violently ill throughout the pregnancy, completely bedridden, and had difficulty even eating. Fisk treated her as best he knew how, and you became healthy, which was her greatest wish. You grew as expected, a thriving young lad who was going to be a great ruler one day, and Kali was so happy, even through her illness. But Kali's body could not handle you.

"Regardless of her illness, somehow Fisk and Kali's physician kept her body alive for the remainder of the pregnancy, or at least, until you were developed enough to be brought forth into the world. It was a grave predicament and a very distressing time for everyone. You must remember, Kata, that superstition surrounding birth is very strong, and it is believed by many that misfortune will befall any mother who is seen by too many questioning eyes when she is heavy with child. So Kali spent much of her pregnancy behind closed doors. Although her absence was very apparent to everyone in the Temple, very few people questioned it. But no matter how careful we were, your birth took Kali's life.

"When finally you were born and Kali died, the Emperor became enraged. His wife was gone, you were a girl, and as everyone knows, girls are not supposed to rule a nation. You were meant to be the pinnacle of greatness, but instead, you were condemned. Kata, you were to be the first Odd child killed.

"But you looked so much like your mother, Kata—you still do. You have her features, her colouring, and as you grew you developed her gentle, inquisitive disposition.

I knew you were mine, of course, and I could not see you murdered, not that I could tell the Emperor that. Instead, I faked your death, even produced the body of an already deceased infant for him to see. Officially, according to all historical documents, the Empress's pregnancy never existed. But in reality, I brought you back to my chamber and raised you as best I could in secrecy."

Low the Wise was weary. He had carried his secret for so long, it had become the reason for his survival. His daughter, so helpless, would not survive without him, and he would not survive if his secret were revealed, for what he had done was a crime against the crown. However, now saying it aloud to his daughter, it was as though a dark shadow within him had faded. Finally, after all those years, he felt a freedom he had never before known.

Katasuma dropped her feet to the floor and sat tall in the grand chair she always sat in, her hands clasped on her lap like a proper lady. "This will be your end, Papa," Katasuma said. "Unless you are able to accept what you did and bring it to rights."

Low looked up at his stately daughter, so much like her regal mother sitting in her throne. "Have you Seen my end then, Kata?" he asked weakly.

Katasuma's expression melted into one of pure affection. "Of course I have, Papa. It was one of the first things I Saw."

Low the Wise nodded, accepting her words. "How will it be then? Hanging?

Decapitation?"

Katasuma's mouth curved into a fetching grin, which caused Low's heart to jerk painfully. "You are very old, Papa," she said instead of answering his question. She tended to be vague like that. "Do you believe what you did was wrong?"

Low barely had to consider his answer. "I believe deceiving your mother was wrong, and I am deeply regretful of it. She believed her child to be the miraculous product of her union with her husband. The first thing I shall do when I see her in the next world is apologize." He paused, considering the rest. "I am not regretful for taking you, though, Kata. That was perhaps the most right thing I have ever done."

Katasuma nodded gently, wise beyond her years. "It is a simple thing then. See your mistakes for what they are then let them go. Learn from them, Papa. You believe your choices were just, and so they were. Do not grieve something that was the right thing to do."

Then Katasuma did something Low was not expecting. For a moment, her hand disappeared into the pocket of her robe, then it reappeared curled around a small stack of parchment. "I made these for you so you can See without me," she said and gave her father the cards.

Low took the papers and turned them over in his hand. On the first, there was a hand-drawn picture of a jovial-looking fool setting out on a voyage to unknown and unfathomable places. He didn't seem at all concerned by the dog biting at his ankles, or the great cliff he was just about to drop from.

"I must take my leap of faith," she said simply. "I cannot stay in these rooms forever. The next time these issues come up, I shall be better prepared."

11

The Fool

♥♦♣♠

Dear Journal,

I can't deny the feeling of familiarity that comes to me each time I go to the witch. Likewise, I can't claim a clear understanding of why I feel so compelled to go to her at all, ridiculous as she is. All I rightly know is that in meeting with her, I feel fulfilled—as if a prophesy has been fulfilled. A foolish notion indeed but one that can't be denied. It's almost like I am stepping away from all that I've ever known and believed in and am taking the great leap I have always dreamed of.

Being an astute man, I am familiar with the concept of reincarnation—the notion that deeds done in one life will effect the next and the next and the next until we are able to transcend our mistakes and finally become released. Although I don't particularly want to admit it to anyone other than you, my dear journal, I can't shake the feeling that somehow I am caught up in an eternal cycle with the witch, as if we know one another from another life. It is a shame, of course, to be tied to someone so dastardly and grisly—a beautiful young woman would have been preferable—but her ugliness keeps my mind sharp, for I do not tend to get tied up in ogling, which frees the mind for thinking. It is not something I can prove, but I feel an eternal connection to her that I cannot break unless I learn and act on some kind of lesson.

I have been considering the idea that people are brought into each other's lives for a purpose. Some call it fate—some kind of synchronicity that cannot be controlled or altered. Although this is not something to be discussed in public, Journal (and I shall never, ever admit it to her!), I have learned much from the witch. Being one of the very few people I have ever met capable of teaching me, clever as I am, I can't help but wonder if she and I were put together for a reason. She is, if nothing else, causing me to think more about the Oddity experiments. She is causing me to do a great deal of things, actually. I am suddenly finding myself questioning the virtue of the experiments.

Due to my recent reading, my morality has become distorted. Is it wrong, for example, for me to consider engineering human beings meant for a specific purpose? Some would say it is, that I am meddling in a place I do not belong and that whatever force it is that created the universe is the only force that ought to dictate human potential. But then I wonder, what is wrong in improving upon that creation if the ability to do so is given to me? Is it not my duty to better our species if at all possible? If I intervene with human creation, am I damning myself to an eternity spent alongside the Devil in the despicable pits of Hell? All I can do is speculate.

I am going to continue pondering these most recent insights, for I do not wish to get into any more trouble than I am already in. I fear, however, that if I don't act, and if I do not present my ideas to the Emperor, my life will become forfeit, which would be such a shame because I am so terribly young, and I am so fond of life. Perhaps, though, if I listen to the witch, if I obey my conscious, I will be expelled from this endless cycle and finally cast into euphoria. The answers I get in death will better prepare me for what lies ahead, which is something I can only guess at, assuming there are any answers to be had.

12

The Hierophant

♥♦♣♠

Low the Wise couldn't say that he was happy to release his daughter into the world, where he was convinced she would meet her doom, however, nor could he deny her the right to leave. With each day that passed, the multitude of ailments, so common in the old, crept angrily in on his otherwise peaceful existence, causing him to worry about her future without him. It was a fact he had spent considerable time thinking about.

The plan was simple: Katasuma would look ahead into the thoughts of whoever was nearby and listen for the decisions they made with regards to which direction they intended to travel and then go the opposite, thereby avoiding confrontation or discovery. She would leave at night, too, knowing there would be fewer people in the corridors to stop her. Low wanted to go with her, at least as far as the Temple doors, but he dared not, for he feared being retained by the gate guards who would undoubtedly refuse his passage, as his station did not favour casual visits to the city proper.

"Although I have given you all that I can, you will need to find employment, Kata," said Low to his daughter shortly before her departure. He considered her pale-skinned face, thinking her quite beautiful, and knew that she would have no trouble at all finding work companioning lonely men. The thought curled his stomach in unpleasant ways, and he sent a silent prayer, asking for her protection.

"I will read futures, Papa," Katasuma said simply. "I will sell people information on their lives, and in that way, I will provide for myself. You needn't worry."

"But what when you have a vision, Kata?" her father reminded her, because it was the events that took place during her visions that had been the cause of her seclusion in the first place. Katasuma's ability might have been easy to hide openly otherwise.

"All part of the act," Katasuma replied. "I've heard that people like eccentric mystics."

Low couldn't deny that it was true—he'd heard much the same—but it didn't settle his nerves any. "You have the papers I prepared for you? You know how to get past the gate guards?"

Katasuma nodded. "Yes, Papa, but what of you when I am gone? How will you maintain your station without my insights?"

Low had put a great deal of consideration into his own future, not because he was selfish, but because he was convinced that if the Emperor noticed his information was increasingly incorrect, he would become suspicious and would either force him to confess, or more likely, have Low dispatched as was his fickle nature. No matter the state or length of their friendship, the Emperor was still likely to act rashly simply because he could.

"I am going to retire, Kata," he answered. "It is high time I did so. Well past high time. Perhaps I will come and join you in your endeavors after some time has passed. Perhaps it will be you who provides for me, old simpleton that I am."

Katasuma nodded, although there was something in the action that seemed superficial, as if she didn't fully believe it would be possible. "You will be welcome with me at any time, Papa," she said simply, "if the new Emperor allows your departure."

As was increasingly apparent to everyone who knew him, the current Emperor was becoming old, too, and thus newly afflicted with various old-timer ailments, such as a great big belly and the preference for simpler occupations—like eating sweets and drinking wine and napping several times per day—rather than ruling. He had no immediate heirs to take over his seat when he died but had begun conditioning his spoiled nephew for the position, who was turning out just as ruthless if not more so than his uncle had been during his reign.

Low, being somewhat grumpy and set in his ways, was in no position to begin again with a new, younger Emperor who would undoubtedly have ideas Low would have no interest in. So, the way he saw it, by retiring now, Low was saving both Emperors the awkwardness of an employment issue. Retirement seemed a welcome rest, if a lonely one.

He would so hate to see his daughter go, but he knew she was right, it was time for her to move on. So, dressed in the common clothing of Temple servants, Katasuma kissed her father's weathered, whiskery cheek, and retreated through the door of his rooms for the first, and the last, time.

13
The Wheel of Fortune

♥♦♣♠

Hanging in the clouds, far, far out of the reach of anything earthly tethered, rotated a great golden wheel. On and about it there were animals—many of them the mystical kind, some with sinister connotations, and some seemingly harmless. It was impossible to tell which way the wheel was turning, if the sphinx was at the top or the snake. Little was clear beyond the feeling of motion, and the recognition that whatever was on the top would not be there for long, and likewise, those who were at the bottom were soon to find themselves at the top.

"The only thing clear about this card is how unclear it is," I said.

The witch grinned, and I found myself becoming concerned by her apparent joy. "That is entirely true. The Wheel of Fortune speaks of balance and the circular pattern of life and death and rebirth. Sometimes, there is no controlling fate, boy. Sometimes we must accept what we are given and learn from it, knowing that in due time, the wheel will turn. But what we must recognize is that nothing is ever gone forever, and each time the wheel presents something, there is something new to learn. It is up to you to see the lesson and to be prepared for whatever outcome awaits you."

It frightened me how clearly I understood her meaning. "With regards to the experiments…"

The witch's expression tightened. "What kind of experiments do you mean, child?"

"Improvement," I answered. "The experiments have to do with improvement." The witch nodded slowly, no trace of cheerfulness left anywhere on her face.

"The Wheel has turned," she said, as if to herself. "There is no denying the changes that are coming—they will come no matter what we do. The only choice we have is whether or not to take all the lessons we have learned and apply them to the change, or to remain ignorant and just go for the ride. What will your choice be, boy?"

The witch's dark eyes were so intense, looking into them was like seeing inside of some undiscovered chasm of the universe.

"My choice?" I pondered the question, for it seemed important to the witch that I answer truthfully. "My choice is simple," I said, although in reality it was anything but. "First, I must face my sins and balance the bad with the good. Then, I shall present my ideas, and see if I will have the opportunity to advance them."

The witch nodded but did not say anything.

"Then, if I am allowed to live, I must consider the betterment of the whole of humanity, without greed, and without suffering. I must be honest with myself and look ahead to the end result. I will not forget any of the steps," I said, because I wanted to show that I understood the witch's lessons.

"And if your plans go awry?"

"I will recognize failure for what it is and accept my fate, because sometimes there is no controlling the future."

The witch gritted together whatever few teeth she had, which both contorted her features and made me feel slightly squeamish from the sound. "We must not fear change—fear is a choice, change is not. But similarly, we must recognize the mistakes of the past and ensure they are not repeated."

I nodded, although I was not at all clear on her meaning.

The witch paused for what seemed an eternity. Then, in a voice that sounded as if it belonged to someone else, she said, "Let me tell you a story, boy, about the time when I was young. My name is Katasuma, and I am the Empress's Oddity daughter."

14

The World

♥♦♣♠

I was not afraid as I walked toward what I knew was going to be the most painful experience of my life. Mind you, I couldn't rightly say that I was looking forward to it either. But I also knew, after all these years, after all I had learned, that there was nothing to fear in endings. For, if I'd learned nothing else, I had learned that in order for there to be a new beginning, there had to first be an ending. I only hoped I'd not make a fool of myself or smell too horribly as I burned.

It had been strange the way things had worked out, but I didn't pretend to understand the mysteries of the universe. Indeed, life was made more exciting when it carried some surprises, or so I believed, and my life had been more exciting than that of many others. It would be sad to let this life go, but I knew that in mourning its loss, I was causing myself to suffer, and that was something I could control. Suffering was of no benefit to me, and besides, I looked goofy with puffy eyes and a heavy heart. No, there was no place for suffering on this day.

I wouldn't go as far as to claim this death a gift, although there are some out there crazy enough to do so, such as the witch who was forever claiming such cockamamie things. The withered, half-baked loon told me that if I chose truth, I'd finally find the ability to break the cycle and transcend my flaws. I really can't agree or disagree with that—it seemed somewhat abstract to me—but I wasn't about to judge, for in letting go and allowing life to progress in the way it naturally wanted to, I have felt a great lightening in my soul. Taking her advice and abandoning the experiments was the right thing to do, even though it has ultimately led to my end.

Flanked on either side by a pair of Imperial buffoons, great thick chains rattling round my ankles and wrists, I shuffle as best I can to the pyre that is to act as the stage for my great disappearing act. There is an enormous crowd gathered, which does my showman's heart proud. If I had the ability to do so, I would bow, for there is nothing grander than accepting praise when praise is due. This death will be one hell of a fine trick.

I had earned myself quite a reputation while travelling with the witch all those years. While she read the futures of those desperate enough to consult her, I developed my own skill as an illusionist, utilizing a mixture of my imagination and the theories I had rejected, to bring forth some truly incredible feats.

My fans adored me, and still do, or so I believe—just look at the numbers that have shown up to see me now. And what's not to love? I can turn a pair of lady's gloves into live doves, convince a length of rope to dance like a snake, and even converse with the dead. Well, that was the best illusion of all, talking to the dead. Really, all it takes is a little research and the ability to eavesdrop, which are skills anyone can learn. Life on the road had been good for me.

When the witch died, old as she was, the feeling was not of sadness—although I had grown quite fond of her over the years—but of completion. She must have felt it too, because the last thing she said to me was, "Finally, the cycle is broken," and I knew she was right. And now I am completing my part, too, by transcending this wheel and moving onto another. I have broken the cycle. I hope to meet the witch again when I am reborn. She was convinced that we had met before during previous cycles, so I have no doubt that I will meet her again.

As a younger man I had earned my salvation because I'd heeded the witch's advice. On the day of my sentence, when asked if I had any final words, I had been honest with the Emperor, appealing to his humanity, ignoring my pride, and admitting to my mistakes, of which there were many. Miraculously, although I was cast from the city and left without my social status, his chief advisor—an old prune of a man—convinced him to grant my relative freedom. The Emperor was not without his own weaknesses, such as a particular fondness for red wine, which helped me greatly on that afternoon, and saw in me a kindred spirit. Then, desperate, disowned by my family and without any place left to go, I returned to the witch, who took me in, for she understood that our destinies were bound to be connected in some way. As time went by and I became accustomed to a showman's life, I became happy, for at least I had no rules beyond those I set for myself. And with that, I was free.

And now I find myself once again facing the end, though this time I will not escape it, and I shall not try to. I stole from the crown, and that is an act worthy of death. But while I may appear to be a thief to all who see me, I will die a martyr, for I believe my death is a lesser price to pay than the alternative.

Although I believe in everyone's right to free speech, I also believe that there is such a thing as the wrong kind of speech, which has the ability to lead to ignorant actions in the weak minded. It was books that I found, books that I stole, and books that I destroyed.

As if they were fated to find their way into my hands, I came across a series of hand written books by someone with the ridiculous name of Fisk, who chose to act upon some theories that were not too unlike many of the ones I'd had in my youth, which is partly why I recognize them as being dangerous.

Contained therein were the means to adjust human composition, explaining a way to give skills to humans that were not meant for us. I know, because of my time with the witch, that such things are possible, for she is a product of such a poorly planned fiasco. But I understand that, while superficially these skills may seem a great benefit to the human species, meddling in human creation does nothing but bring terribly blinding greed upon the creators and unhappiness to those afflicted. And that's not to mention the possibility of mass destruction on an almost biblical scale, for I know what the witch said about responsibility is true. Such powers in the wrong hands could lead to disaster.

The witch, Katasuma, had been forced to live her life a lonely soul, never finding true happiness and never reaching her potential. Being able to See the future had not allowed her the life she deserved but made her an outcast, seen as a threat and forever hunted. She was perpetually afraid of saying the wrong thing to the wrong person, which resulted in her frayed nerves and seclusion, for she would not allow herself to become spiritually close to anyone. I believe, as did Katasuma, that if we were meant to See the future, we would naturally have the ability to do so. So, I destroyed the books, and now I will be destroyed because of it. See? I'm a martyr.

I have been dressed in white robes, which was a poor choice for I look ridiculous in such washed-out colours. If the choice had been mine, I might have preferred royal blue or blood red, even. Yes red would have been spectacular. My hair has been shorn, which is truly a misery, for the baldness of my tender scalp is itchy, and I have always had such a marvelous coiffure. But, just like the rest of my physical form, the loss of my hair no longer matters, for soon I will leave it and everything else behind. I have been working on conquering my vanity, but it is such a difficult thing. It is one of my few remaining flaws—if not for my vanity, I'd be perfect.

My escorts heft me onto the platform that is raised above the majority of the brambles to allow the witnesses a better view. I smile in the most fetching manner, sure to flash the ladies my finely spaced row of teeth. I don't care that the gesture likely looks more like a sneer, for perhaps it is a bit, considering their fickle hearts. It is almost funny, but after all this time, I still don't understand women.

Preparing for the pain, I close my eyes and summon the most complete calm I can manage, which is surprisingly quite considerable. I focus as best I can on my mental form, trying to systematically shut down my physical one. I listen to the sound of my blood pumping rapidly through my body and consciously try to slow it. I bring my awareness to my breathing, which is continuing in a steady rhythm. I hear the great crack and sizzle as the fiery torch is brought to the sticks and rubbish near my feet; the fire's immediate ferocity quite impressive. But that is all I hear of the world around me. I am nearly out of my body now.

I feel the pain in my toes, which truly is excruciating, but I focus on my lungs instead, for it is air I need to preserve, and air is about to become a very costly commodity. I fill my lungs to their capacity and beyond, the tight expansion in my chest most disagreeable. I push forcefully at the breath within me, becoming drunk on it. I feel the pressure in my head first, my mind becoming full of the night sky and stars though I am not clear-headed enough to recognize its beauty. My fingers begin to vibrate with it, my toes, too, moving without my intervention.

I would have laughed if laughing weren't so wasteful, for it is becoming apparent to me that I really am disappearing. I can see the universe in my head and know

I am in the process of joining with it. There will be no less of me when I leave this world, I will simply be more spread out. Diluted, as the witch called it.

The pain truly is exemplary as I force the air through the pores of my skin, pushing the spaces apart. The sensation travels up my legs and arms, slowly, perhaps too slowly, it is difficult to tell. My awareness becomes light as my flesh lifts off my bones and dissipates back into the air, transforming back into the dust from which it came. I slow the beating of my heart, focusing on its stagnancy but living on anyway. Then, with my last remaining energy, I push myself apart, my particles taking to the air disguised as smoke and ashes.

And I know without question that I am free.

Acknowledgements

Thank you to all my darlings, whom I have not killed despite William Faulkner's advice. Thank you to all my darlings who have not killed me despite likely wanting to. Thank you to Kirsten, who is a darling that deserves extra thanking due to her ability to perform magic. Thank you to Wesley, Marcus, and Jackson who have taught me the close relation between insanity and genius. Thank you to Brad for being alive. Thank you to my mom and dad, who are my biggest fans. Thank you to everyone else who has touched this story in any way, weather they know it or not. Thanks and thanks and thanks.